The Little Rabbit
Who Wanted Red Wings

By Carolyn Sherwin Bailey Illustrated by Chris Santoro

BARNES
&NOBLE
B O O K S
N E W   Y O R K

1997 Barnes & Noble Books   ISBN 0-7607-0634-4
97 98 99 00 01 M 9 8 7 6 5 4 3 2 1
LFA

Once there was a Little Rabbit who had soft pink ears, bright red eyes, and a short, fluffy tail. He was such a cute little rabbit. But he wasn't happy. He wanted to be somebody else instead of the nice little rabbit that he was.

Whenever Mr. Bushy Tail the gray squirrel passed by, the Little Rabbit would say to his mommy, "Oh, Mommy! I wish I had a long gray tail like Mr. Bushy Tail's."

And when Mr. Porcupine passed by, the Little Rabbit would say to his mommy, "Oh, Mommy! I wish I had a back full of bristles like Mr. Porcupine's."

And whenever Mrs. Puddle-Duck passed by in her two red rubbers, the Little Rabbit would say to his mommy, "Oh, Mommy! I wish I had a pair of red rubbers like Mrs. Puddle-Duck's."

One day, Old Mr. Groundhog heard the Little Rabbit wishing. Old Mr. Groundhog was very wise indeed, so he said to the Little Rabbit, "Why don't you go down to the wishing pond? If you look at yourself in the water and turn around three times, your wish will come true."

So the Little Rabbit trotted off all alone through the woods, until he came to a pool of green water lying in a low tree stump. That was the wishing pond.

Beside the wishing pond sat a small red bird, drinking happily. As soon as the Little Rabbit saw him, he began to wish again. "Oh," he said to himself, "I wish I had a pair of red wings."

Just then he looked in the wishing pond and saw his little face. Then he turned around three times and something happened. The Little Rabbit began to have a strange feeling in his shoulders, like he had in his mouth when his teeth were growing in. It was his wings coming through.

So he sat all day in the woods by the wishing pond, waiting for his wings to grow. By and by, just before sundown, he started home to show his mommy his beautiful pair of long red wings.

It was dark when the Little Rabbit reached home. He knocked on the door. His mother opened it immediately, but she didn't know him. No, she really and truly did not know him. For she had never seen a little rabbit with red wings before!

The Little Rabbit had no choice but to go looking for a place to spend the night, because his mommy would not let him get into his own bed. After a while he came upon Mr. Bushy Tail's house. He rapped on the door and said, "Please, kind Mr. Bushy Tail, may I sleep in your house all night?" But as soon as Mr. Bushy Tail saw the strange rabbit, he slammed the door shut. He had never seen a little rabbit with red wings in all his life.

The Little Rabbit went on until he came to Mrs. Puddle-Duck's nest down by the marsh. "Please, kind Mrs. Puddle-Duck," he said, "may I sleep in your nest all night?"

But Mrs. Puddle-Duck poked her head out of the nest just a little way. "No, no, no," she said. "Go away." For she, too, had never seen such an odd-looking rabbit in all her life.

So the Little Rabbit went on and on until he came to Old Mr. Groundhog's hole. Wise Old Mr. Groundhog recognized him at once and let him spend the night. But the hole had beechnuts spread all over it. And while that pleased Old Mr. Groundhog, the beechnuts made the Little Rabbit very uncomfortable. He had a terrible night.

By morning the Little Rabbit was in despair and he began to cry for his mommy. Old Mr. Groundhog, knowing the time was right, said to his little friend:

"Do you still want your red wings?"

"No, no!" said the Little Rabbit.

"Well, then," said Mr. Groundhog, "why don't you go down to the wishing pond and wish them off again?"

Immediately, the Little Rabbit scampered off to the wishing pond and saw his face in it. Then he turned around three times, and sure enough, his red wings got smaller and smaller until they were gone altogether.

The Little Rabbit went straight home to his mommy. She knew him right away and was overjoyed to see the little rabbit that she loved. And the Little Rabbit never, ever wished to be somebody other than himself.

The End